Rapunzel

and other
stories

First published in 2002 by Miles Kelly Publishing,
Bardfield Centre, Great Bardfield, Essex CM7 4SL

24681097531

Copyright © Miles Kelly Publishing Ltd 2002

Project manager: Paula Borton
Editorial Assistant: Nicola Sail

British Library Cataloguing-in-Publication Data
A catalogue record for this book is available from the British Library

ISBN 1-84236-091-4

Printed in Hong Kong

Visit us on the web:
www.mileskelly.net
Info@mileskelly.net

Rapunzel

and other stories

Chosen by Fiona Waters

Miles Kelly
PUBLISHING

Contents

The Seven Ravens

a fairytale from Poland

There was once a poor widow who had seven great sons and a daughter. The daughter, Anne, was a good girl, but the seven brothers were wild as the hills. One day the widow was baking a blackberry pie. As she rolled out the pastry the whole noisy troop came shouting into the kitchen.

"Blackberry pie!" they yelled. "When will it be ready?"

"When it is cooked," she said crossly. "Let me finish then we can all eat." But the boys just ran about the hot kitchen, pushing and shoving each other and leaving great muddy bootmarks all over the clean floor.

"Oh, can't you be quiet! I wish, I wish you were ravens instead of great noisy boys," she cried. But then her eyes widened in horror as the boys shrank, and feathers covered their arms. Their mouths turned into beaks, and with seven deep croaks they flew out of the door. Anne rushed to the window, but the ravens were already out of sight. Together mother and daughter sat weeping, and not even the smell of burning pie could rouse them.

But the next day Anne said to her mother, "I am determined to find my brothers and bring them safely back home."

So she set off with nothing but her needle and thread

and scissors in her pocket. She walked and walked and came across a curious little house in the woods. It was made of silver, and the woman who opened the door was dressed in a long silver robe. But she was not friendly.

"I am all behind today, and my husband will be home soon. There is no supper ready, and I have to mend his cloak," she said all in a rush.

"I could mend the cloak," said Anne taking out her needle, "and then you can cook the supper."

Well, the woman was delighted and opened the door wide. Anne sat quietly in the corner and with the tiniest stitches ever mended the beautiful cloak. When the husband, who was also dressed all in silver, came in he was very impressed with Anne's work, and invited her to join them for supper which was the most delicious roast chicken.

The silver man asked Anne where she was going so she told them the whole story of her brothers.

"Perhaps we can help you," said the silver man. "We are the moon's helpers and she sees most things on earth. I will ask her if she knows where your brothers are."

As the wife cleared the table after supper, she gave Anne the chicken bones.

"Keep these in your pocket, you never know when they might come in useful," and Anne did so.

When the silver man returned the next morning he told Anne that the moon had seen seven ravens flying round the Amber Mountain. When Anne asked him where the Amber Mountain was he told her to follow her nose until she could go no further. Anne thanked the silver couple and set off once again, her nose very firmly in front.

After several days she came to a halt. There in front of her was the Amber Mountain, its sides steep as glass. Anne did not know what to do, but then she remembered the chicken bones. She pushed one into the surface of the mountain and stood on it. Then she put the second bone in a little higher, and stood on that, and so she slowly, slowly climbed to the very top of the mountain. And there she found seven sad-looking ravens. They were her brothers! But there was also an evil old witch sitting there too.

"Well, my dear, your brothers are under my spell, and the only way you can release them is by remaining silent for seven years. Not one single word or you will lose them for ever," and with an evil cackle she flew off.

Anne climbed down the mountain, and when she reached home her mother was delighted to see her. But Anne could tell her nothing. Four years passed in silence until one day Anne was out gathering firewood when a royal hunting party came through the wood. The prince was very struck by Anne's quiet ways, but of course he couldn't get a word out of her. Thereafter he came by every day, and at length asked her to marry him. She smiled her acceptance but never a word did she utter.

Three more years passed, and the prince and Anne had a baby son. Now the queen had never really approved of her son marrying such a poor girl, however pretty she might be, and she never lost an opportunity to make mischief. One day she rushed into the prince and accused Anne of trying to poison the baby. The prince was horrified but, of course, when he asked Anne if she had done such a terrible

thing, she was unable to reply. So he sent her to the
dungeons, and told her she had three days to explain herself
or she would die.

The three days passed with Anne still not uttering a
word. On the third day, she was brought out into the
courtyard where everyone waited to see what would
happen next.

Suddenly there was a great flapping of wings and seven

ravens landed in a circle around Anne. It was her brothers, and in a blink of an eye there they stood, restored to human shape. Well, you can imagine what a lot Anne had to tell! They all talked into the night. The queen had somehow gone missing, but no one seemed to mind too much. The seven brothers went to collect their mother, and when they all came back together the prince promised her that she would never have to do a day's work again!

The Twelve Dancing Princesses

a retelling from the original story by the Brothers Grimm

The king was very puzzled. He had twelve daughters, each one as beautiful as the moon and the stars, and he loved them above all the riches in his kingdom. But every morning the princesses would appear yawning and bleary-eyed, and with their shoes worn quite through. Every evening the king would kiss them good night and lock the door behind him. So how did they get out? And where did they go? The princesses certainly were not letting on.

Buying new shoes every day was costing him a fortune so the king determined to solve the mystery. The court messenger was sent to all four corners of the kingdom to issue the king's proclamation that he would give the hand of one of his daughters in marriage to any man who could discover the secret. But should he fail after three nights he would be banished forever.

Needless to say there were plenty of young men willing to risk banishment to win such a prize. But they soon found the princesses were too clever by half. Before they retired for the night, the princesses sang and played their musical instruments and fed them sweetmeats and rich honeyed mead. Before they realised it morning had come and there were the sleepy princesses and twelve pairs of worn-out shoes.

The king was beside himself. Only the court shoemaker went about with a smile on his face.

Now into the kingdom at this time there wandered a penniless soldier. He read the proclamation and had just decided to try his luck when an old woman came slowly down the dusty road. The young man offered her some of his bread and cheese, and as they sat peaceably together the old woman asked where he was bound. When he had explained she said, "Well, I may be able to help you. You must not drink the mead those cunning princesses offer you, for it is drugged. Pretend to be asleep, and you shall see what you shall see. This may help you," and the old woman handed him a silvery cloak. "Whenever you wear this you will be invisible. Use it well!" and the old woman disappeared.

"Well, perhaps I will succeed now I have magic on my side," murmured the young man as he set off for the palace. By now the king was tearing his hair out. The court shoemaker had taken on extra cobblers to help keep up with the demand for new shoes every day. The princesses were falling asleep into their bowls of porridge at breakfast every morning.

The young man bowed deeply to the king and smiled at all the princesses. He ate a hearty supper but when the eldest princess gave him a goblet of mead he only pretended to drink it. Then he yawned loudly and let his head droop as if he had fallen asleep.

The butler and the first footman dumped the young

man onto the bed placed
across the door of the
princesses' bedchamber. He
cautiously opened one eye
and gazed around the
room. The princesses were
putting on gorgeous velvet
and brocade dresses
and rings and
necklaces. They
giggled and
whispered as they
brushed their hair,
powdered their faces
and then pulled on
the brand new
jewelled slippers

that the shoemaker had only delivered a few hours earlier.
The eldest princess clapped her hands three times. A trap
door opened up in the floor and they all swiftly descended
down a steeply curving staircase. Just as soon as the last
princess had disappeared the young man flung the magic
cloak round his shoulders and rushed after them.

He found himself in a wondrous garden where the trees
were covered in rich jewels, sparkling in candlelight.
Musicians played whirling tunes and he saw all the
princesses dancing with the most handsome princes. The

young man was spellbound, but he managed to keep his wits about him. He reached up and broke off a branch from one of the jewelled trees and hid it under his cloak. Then he ran back and lay down on his bed as though he had never stirred. So it happened on the second and the third nights.

It was with a weary voice that the king asked the young man at breakfast on the fourth day if he had found out where the princesses went at night. The king sat up very quickly when the young man told his tale and produced the branches from the trees. The king was delighted and the young man chose the youngest sister for his bride. And they all lived happily ever after. Except, of course, the court shoemaker, who always made the young man's shoes just a little too tight so they pinched.

Rapunzel

a retelling from the original fairytale by the Brothers Grimm

Once upon a time there lived a man and his wife who for years and years had wanted a child. One day the wife was looking sadly out of the window. Winter was coming but in the next door garden, which was surrounded by a huge great wall, she could just see rows and rows of delicious vegetables. In particular, she could see a huge bunch of rapunzel, a special kind of lettuce. Her mouth watered, it looked so fresh and green.

"Husband, I shall not rest until I have some of that rapunzel growing next door," she whispered.

The husband clambered over the wall and quickly picked a small bunch which he took back to his wife. She made it into a salad, and ate it all up. But the next day, all she could think of was how delicious it had been so she asked him to pick her some more.

He clambered over the wall again, and was picking a small bunch of the rapunzel when a voice behind him hissed, "So you are the one who has been stealing my rapunzel!"

When he spun round, there stood a witch and she looked very angry indeed. The husband was terrified, but he tried to explain that his wife had been

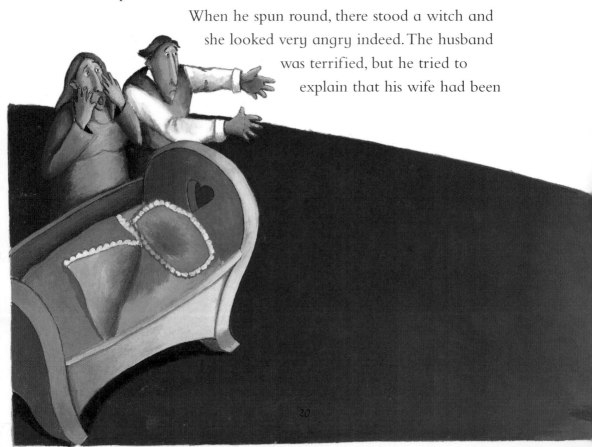

desperate for some fresh leaves for her salad.

"You may take all the leaves you require then, but you must give me your first child when she is born," smiled the witch, and it was not a nice smile. The husband was greatly relieved, however, for he knew that there was little chance of his wife ever having a daughter so he fled back over the wall, clutching the bunch of rapunzel. He did not tell his wife of his meeting with the witch for he thought it would only frighten her, and he soon forgot all about his adventure.

But it all came back to him when nine months later his wife gave birth to a beautiful baby girl. No sooner had she laid the baby in her cradle, than the witch appeared to claim the child. The wife wept, the husband pleaded but nothing could persuade the witch to forget the husband's awful promise, and so she took the tiny baby away.

The witch called the baby Rapunzel.
She grew into a beautiful girl with long,
long hair as fine as spun gold. When she
was sixteen, the witch took Rapunzel
and locked her into a tall tower so no
one would see how beautiful she
was. The witch threw away the
key to the tower, and so whenever
she wanted to visit Rapunzel she would
call out, "Rapunzel, Rapunzel, let down your hair,"
and Rapunzel would throw her golden plait of hair
out of the window at the top of the tower so the witch
could slowly scramble up.

Now one day it happened that a handsome young
prince was riding through the woods. He heard the
witch call out to Rapunzel and he watched her climb
up the tower. After the witch had gone, the prince came
to the bottom of the tower and he called up, "Rapunzel,
Rapunzel, let down your hair," and he climbed quickly up
the shining golden plait. You can imagine Rapunzel's
astonishment when she saw the handsome Prince standing
in front of her but she was soon laughing at his stories.
When he left, he promised to come again the next day, and
he did. And the next, and the next, and soon they had fallen
in love with each other.

One day as the witch clambered up Rapunzel

exclaimed, "You are slow! The prince doesn't take nearly as long to climb up the tower," but no sooner were the words out of her mouth than she realised her terrible mistake. The witch seized the long, long golden plait and cut it off. She drove Rapunzel far, far away from the tower, and then sat down to await the prince. When the witch heard him calling, she threw the golden plait out of the window. Imagine the prince's dismay when he sprang into the room only to discover the horrible witch instead of his beautiful Rapunzel! When the witch told him he would never see his Rapunzel again, in his grief he flung himself out of the

tower. He fell into some brambles which scratched his eyes so he could no longer see.

And thus he wandered the land, always asking if anyone had seen his Rapunzel. After seven long years, he came to the place where she had hidden herself away. As he stumbled down the road, Rapunzel recognised him and with a great cry of joy she ran up to him and took him gently by the hand to her little cottage in the woods. As she washed his face, two of her tears fell on the prince's eyes and his sight came back. And so they went back to his palace and lived happily ever after. The witch, you will be pleased to hear, had not been able to get down from the tower, so she did NOT live happily ever after!

Teeny–Tiny

an English folk tale

O nce upon a time there lived a teeny-tiny old woman. She lived in a teeny-tiny house in a teeny-tiny street with a teeny-tiny cat. One day the teeny-tiny woman decided to go out for a teeny-tiny walk. She put on her teeny-tiny boots and her teeny-tiny bonnet, and off she set.

When she had walked a teeny-tiny way down the teeny-tiny street, she went through a teeny-tiny gate into a teeny-tiny graveyard, which was a teeny-tiny shortcut to the teeny-tiny meadow. Well, she had only taken a few teeny-tiny steps when she saw a teeny-tiny bone lying on

top of a teeny-tiny grave. She thought that would do very well to make some teeny-tiny soup for supper so she put the teeny-tiny bone in her teeny-tiny pocket and went home at once to her teeny-tiny house.

Now the teeny-tiny woman was tired when she reached her teeny-tiny house so she did not make the teeny-tiny soup immediately but put the teeny-tiny bone into her teeny-tiny cupboard. Then she sat in her teeny-tiny chair and put her teeny-tiny feet up and had a teeny-tiny sleep. But she had only been asleep a teeny-tiny time when she woke up at the sound of a teeny-tiny voice coming from her teeny-tiny cupboard. The teeny-tiny voice said, "Where is my teeny-tiny bone?"

Well, the teeny-tiny woman was a teeny-tiny bit frightened so she wrapped her teeny-tiny shawl round her teeny-tiny head and went to sleep again. She had only been asleep a teeny-tiny time when the teeny-tiny voice came from the teeny-tiny cupboard again, a teeny-tiny bit louder this time. "Where is my teeny-tiny bone?"

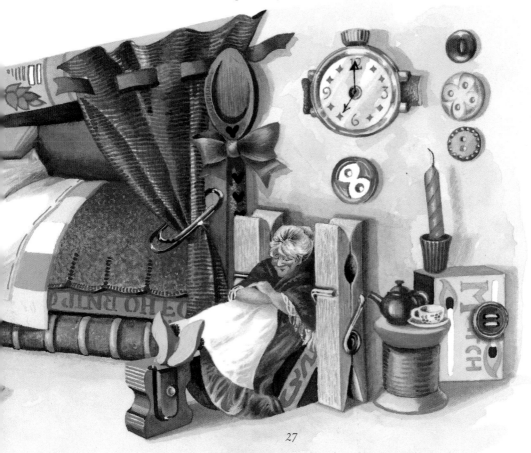

The teeny-tiny woman was a teeny-tiny bit more frightened than last time so she hid under the teeny-tiny cushions, but she could not go back to sleep, not even a teeny-tiny bit. Then the teeny-tiny voice came again and this time it was even a teeny-tiny bit louder. "Where is my teeny-tiny bone?"

This time the teeny-tiny woman sat up in her teeny-tiny chair and said in her loudest teeny-tiny voice, "TAKE IT!"

There was a teeny-tiny silence, and then a teeny-tiny ghost ran out of the teeny-tiny house, down the teeny-tiny street, through the teeny-tiny gate into the teeny-tiny graveyard – with the teeny-tiny bone clutched very tightly in its teeny-tiny hand! And the teeny-tiny woman never took even a teeny-tiny walk there ever again!

East of the Sun and West of the Moon

a retelling from Popular Tales from the Norse by George Webbe Dasent

Once there was a poor herdsman and his wife who lived in a tumbledown cottage in the north of the country with their family. There were seven sons and six daughters and the youngest daughter was the best of the lot.

One cold winter's night there came a gentle knock at the door. When the herdsman opened it, to his surprise there was a Great Brown Bear outside.

"Herdsman, I would be grateful if you would give me your youngest daughter," said the Brown Bear very politely. "If you do, I shall make you rich beyond belief."

This was a tempting offer, but the herdsman thought he should ask his daughter first. She said, "NO!" very loudly.

But the rest of the family persuaded her that the Brown Bear looked kind enough, and they really could do with the money. So she brushed her hair and put on her cloak, and

off she went with the Brown
Bear.

"Get on my back, and
hold onto my fur tightly," said
the Brown Bear, and she did.
They rode a long way to a
great castle. The Brown Bear
galloped in through the front
door, and there was a table laid
with a delicious-looking meal.
The Brown Bear gave the
daughter a silver bell saying,

"Whatever you want, just ring the bell and it shall be
yours," and he padded away silently.

Well, the youngest daughter ate till she was full and
then all she could wish for was a good sleep. So she rang
the silver bell, and she found herself in a warm room with a
great four poster bed. No sooner had she snuggled down in
the warm soft blankets and blown out the candle than she
felt something lie across her feet. It was the Brown Bear. But
when she woke in the morning he had gone. She rang her
bell for breakfast and then spent a very happy day
wandering round the castle.

And so she settled down to life in the Brown Bear's
castle. But after a while she grew sad. She missed her family.
So the Brown Bear offered to take her home for a visit. But
he warned her, "Whatever you do, you must not spend time
alone with your mother. If you do, there is no telling what

bad luck will follow."

She promised and they both set off.
The Brown Bear bounded over the snow,
and it seemed no time before she was
once again with her family. They now
lived in a grand house with many
rooms and a servant for everyone.
They all thanked her for making
their lives so much happier.

Her mother said, "Now, my
daughter, you must tell me all
about your new life!" and she
led her away from the rest of the
family. The youngest daughter quite forgot
her promise to the Brown Bear and she was soon telling her
mother everything. When she came to the bit about the
Brown Bear sleeping across her feet every night, her mother
let out a great shriek.

"Foolish child! This bear must be a troll in disguise! You
must wait until he is asleep, and then take a good look at
him. Then you will see what he really is."

So when the Brown Bear had taken her home again,
the youngest daughter did as her mother suggested. As she
held the candle high above the bed she saw not a sleeping
bear, not even a troll, but the most handsome prince ever.
But, as she bent closer, some wax fell from the candle onto
his shirt and he awoke with a start.

"Alas!" he cried. "What have you done? Had you only

waited, you might have released me from the wicked witch whose spell has turned me into a bear by day. Now I must return to her castle which is East O' the Sun and West O' the Moon, and marry the princess with the three-foot nose."

The prince looked at her once more, his eyes full of tears, and with a rumble of thunder he disappeared. As did the castle and the gardens. The youngest daughter found herself alone in the middle of a forest.

"Well, it is my fault that I have lost the prince so I will just have to try to find him again and rescue him," she said to herself, and she set off to find the castle East O' the Sun and West O' the Moon.

She had walked for seven days and seven nights when she met an old woman sitting by the roadside. The old woman had a golden apple in her lap.

"Do you know where I might find the castle East O' the Sun and West O' the Moon?" the girl asked.

The old woman replied, "No, but my sister might. You can borrow my horse, he will lead you to her. You better take this apple with you, too."

The horse galloped through the night for
seven days until they saw an old,
old woman sitting by the
roadside. The old, old woman
had a golden comb.

"Do you know where I
might find the castle East O' the
Sun and West O' the Moon?" the
girl asked.

The old, old woman replied,
"No, but my sister might. You can
borrow my horse, he will lead you
to her. You better take this comb
with you, too."

The horse galloped through the night for seven days
until they saw an old, old, old woman by the roadside. The
old, old, old woman had a golden spinning wheel.

"Do you know where I might find the castle East O'
the Sun and West O' the Moon?" the girl asked.

The old, old, old woman replied, "No, but the East
Wind will. You can borrow my horse, he will lead you to
him. You better take this spinning wheel with you, too."

The horse galloped through the night for seven days
until they found the East Wind. He didn't know where the
castle was. He suggested the girl try his brother the West
Wind and he blew her all the way to the West Wind's house.
But he didn't know where the castle was either. So the West

Wind suggested she try his
brother the South Wind, but
when they reached the South
Wind's house he was fast
asleep.

"I think you need to try my
brother the North Wind, but he is
very busy and very fierce," said the
West Wind, and he blew her a long,
long way to the top of a bleak mountain. There they
met the North Wind.

"Do you know where I might find the castle East O'
the Sun and West O' the Moon?" the girl asked.

"Indeed I do," howled the
North Wind. "I will take you
there," and with a mighty gust he
blew the girl and the golden
apple and the golden comb and
the golden spinning wheel until
they reached the castle East O'
the Sun and West O' the Moon.

The girl sat down outside
the castle and began to throw
the golden apple high up into
the air. A window was flung open and there stood the
princess, her three-foot nose resting on the window edge.

"What do you want for your golden apple?" she
shrieked down and her voice was like a saw.

"To spend the evening with the prince," replied the girl.

Well, that was easily arranged, but when she went into his chamber, the youngest daughter found the prince fast asleep. The witch had given him a sleeping draught so the youngest daughter went sadly away.

The next morning the girl sat combing her hair with the golden comb, and it was the same story. The princess with the three-foot nose took the golden comb, but again the prince just slept and slept.

The third morning, the youngest daughter sat outside with the golden spinning wheel, and again the princess stuck her great nose out of the window. But this time, the prince's little page told the prince all about the girl who had tried to wake him the nights before, so when the witch brought him his cocoa he only pretended to drink it.

When the youngest daughter came in, he was awake and waiting for her. As soon as he saw her, the prince was overjoyed and kissed her. Straightaway, there was a terrible shriek from the tower at the top of the castle as the witch disappeared in a flash of green light. The princess found her nose was three-foot longer again, so she ran away to hide and was never seen again.

The prince married the youngest daughter the very next day, and the castle East O' the Sun and West O' the Moon became a happy place. Even the North Wind blew more gently round the battlements.

Why the Robin has a
Red Breast

an Inuit legend

In the land where it is always winter all the time, there once lived a man and his son. It was so cold that they lived in a house made of snow, and their clothes were all made of fur.

But even with the warm furs it was cold in the snow house. The man and his son needed a fire as well. They needed it to heat the snow house. They needed it to have hot food to eat. So they could never let their fire go out as without it they would surely die.

Whenever the father went out hunting, he would leave his son with a great pile of wood. The fire burned brightly by the entrance to the snow house. The first thing the boy had learned was never ever to let the fire go out.

Now one of the creatures the man was always hunting was the great white bear. The great white bear hated the man and used all his cunning to hide from the hunter. The bear saw that the fire was precious to the man and his son. He thought that if only he could stamp out the fire with his huge white paws, the man and his son would fall into such a deep cold sleep that they would never wake again. So the great white bear watched and waited for his chance.

One day the father fell ill. All day he tossed and turned on his bed. He was not able to go out hunting. The great white bear watched as the son fed the fire with sticks as his father had taught him. The next day, the father was no better. The son looked after him as well as he could but by now he was growing hungry. At night he could hear the great white bear prowling round the snow house, and he was afraid. The third day the father hardly moved at all, and the boy had to fight to keep his eyes open. He put some more sticks onto the fire, but eventually he could keep his eyes open no longer. He fell into a deep, deep sleep.

The great white bear pounced. He stomped and stamped and put the fire out with his huge white paws. Then he padded away, leaving the boy and his father to their fate. It grew bitterly cold in the snow house. Frost and snow gathered round the furs on the bed, and round the boy's furry hood. Still he slept on and on. Both father and son grew stiff with cold.

The boy had one special friend. It was a tiny little brown bird called a robin. The boy used to feed the robin and let it shelter in the snow house when the blizzards blew. The little bird came hopping up to the snow house and he saw right away that all was not well. He twittered round the boy's head, calling to warn him that the fire had gone out. But still the boy slept on, exhausted by all his efforts to look after his father. The robin scratched among the ashes where the great white bear had stomped, desperately looking for just one tiny ember that was still alight. He found one tiny spark, and he began fanning it with his little wings. He flapped his wings for all he was worth and slowly, slowly the flame caught. It spread to another piece of stick, and still the robin flapped and flapped his wings.

The heat was growing now, and the robin's feathers were scorching. More and more sticks caught alight, and the brave little robin felt his chest feathers burn red with heat.

The boy woke with a start and leapt to his feet. He saw the fire was nearly out, and he rushed to pile on more sticks. He did not see his tiny friend flutter off into the darkness outside. It grew warmer in the snow house, and to his great joy the boy saw his father was stirring on the bed. His eyes were clear and the sickness had passed. In the distance, the great white bear stumped off a long way from the snow house. He could see he was not going to get the better of the hunter and his son.

The next time the robin came to the snow house for food, the boy was puzzled to see the little brown bird now had a bright red breast. But he was never to know why.

The Frog Prince

a retelling from the original story by the Brothers Grimm

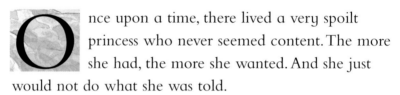

O nce upon a time, there lived a very spoilt
princess who never seemed content. The more
she had, the more she wanted. And she just
would not do what she was told.

One day she took her golden ball out into the woods,
although she had been told by her chief nanny that she
must embroider some new handkerchiefs. She threw the
golden ball high up into the sky once, twice, but the third
time it slipped from her hands and, with a great splash, it
fell down, down into a deep well. The princess stamped her
foot and yelled, but this did not help. So she kicked the side
of the well, and was just getting ready for another big yell,
when a very large frog plopped out of the well.

"Ugh!" said the princess. "A horrible slimy frog, go

away at once," but the frog didn't move. Instead, it spoke.

"What are you making such a fuss about?"

A talking frog! For a moment the princess was speechless, but then she looked down her nose and said,

"If you must know, my most precious golden ball has fallen down this well, and I want it back."

With a sudden leap, the frog disappeared down the well. In the wink of an eye, it was back with the golden ball. The princess went to snatch it up, but the frog put a wet foot rather firmly on it and said,

"Hasn't anyone taught you any manners? 'Please' and 'thank you' would not go amiss, and anyway I have a special request to make."

The princess looked at the frog in utter astonishment. No one ever dared talk to her like that, and certainly not a frog. She glared at the frog and said crossly,

"May I have my ball back, please, and what is your special request?"

The frog did not move its foot, but bent closer to the princess.

"I want to come and live with you in the palace and

eat off your plate and sleep on your pillow, please."

The princess looked horrified, but she was sure a promise to a frog wouldn't count so she shrugged her shoulders and said, "Course you can," and grabbed her golden ball from under the frog's foot and ran back to the palace very quickly.

That night at supper the royal family heard a strange voice calling,

"Princess, where are you?" and in hopped the frog.

"Oh bother!" said the princess. The queen fainted. The king frowned.

"Do you know this frog, princess?" he asked.

"Oh bother!" said the princess again, but she had to tell her father what had happened. When he heard the story, he insisted the princess keep her promise.

The frog ate very little, the princess even less. And when it was time to go to bed, the king just looked very sternly at the princess who was trying to sneak off on her own. She bent down and picked the frog up by one leg, and when she reached her great four-poster bed, she plonked the frog down in the farthest corner. She did not sleep a wink all night.

The next evening, the frog was back. Supper was a quiet affair. The queen stayed in her room, the king read the newspaper, and the princess tried not to look at the frog. Bedtime came, and once again the frog and the princess slept at opposite ends of the bed.

The third evening, the princess was terribly hungry so she just pretended the frog was not there and ate everything

that was placed in front of her. When it came to bedtime, she was so exhausted that she fell in a deep sleep as soon as her head touched the pillow.

The next morning when she woke up, she felt much better for her good sleep until she remembered the frog. But it was nowhere to be seen. At the foot of the bed, however, there stood a very handsome young man in a green velvet suit.

"Hello, princess. Do you know that you snore?" he said.

The princess's mouth fell open ready to yell, but the handsome young man continued, "I don't suppose you

recognise me, thank goodness, but I was the frog who
rescued your golden ball. I was bewitched by a fairy who
said I was rude and spoilt," and here the young man looked
sideways at the princess whose mouth was still hanging
open, "And the spell could only be broken by someone
equally rude and spoilt having to be nice to me."

The princess closed her mouth. The king was most
impressed with the young man's good manners, and the
queen liked the look of his fine green velvet suit. Everyone
liked the fact that the princess had become a very much
nicer person. Before long it seemed sensible for the princess
and the handsome young man to get married. They had
lots of children who were not at all spoilt and everyone
lived happily ever after. The golden ball and the green
velvet suit were put away in a very dark cupboard.

Kaatje's Treasure

a myth from Holland

Hans was a cheesemaker and he lived with his wife Kaatje. They had a small farm near the crossroads by the Old Inn outside the Dutch town of Haarlem. Every week Hans would go to market in Amsterdam with his great big round cheeses, and he would come back with some coins jingling in his pocket, and a few bulbs for his wife to plant in her little garden. Kaatje was a dreamer but Hans loved her very much.

One day as Hans was pressing the cheeses in the dairy, he noticed Kaatje was not singing as usual.

"What is wrong, my dear?" he asked. "You are not as happy as usual."

"Oh, husband, I have had a very strange dream three nights running now. It was so real!" she whispered.

"You and your dreams," laughed Hans. "Tell me what happened then."

So Kaatje told him that she had dreamt she must go to Amsterdam and then walk round the Corn Exchange three times. From then on she would be rich beyond her wildest dreams. Hans thought it was another of her daft wishes, but she was very serious so eventually he agreed to walk round the Corn Exchange three times when he next went to market with his cheeses. And so Kaatje would have to wait until market day. She simply couldn't wait that long so she crept out of the house very early the next morning while Hans was still asleep, and set off on the road to Amsterdam.

She walked and walked, and then some more and eventually she arrived in Amsterdam. She was very excited as she set off round the Corn Exchange. Once. Twice. And a final third time. Absolutely nothing happened. Kaatje sat down with a thump. Her feet were very sore. Her head ached. And she felt very silly. Whatever would Hans say when he heard where she had been. Her eyes filled with tears.

"Can I help you?" a kindly voice said. "You seem to be lost, I have watched you walk three times round the Corn Exchange."

Kaatje looked up and there was a man,

a farmer by he look of him, and he had such a kindly face that before too long Kaatje was telling him her silly dream. Well, he just laughed and laughed.

"I had a dream like that once, but I knew it was only a dream," the farmer said. "I dreamt I had to go to the dairy of a small farm near the crossroads by the Old Inn outside the Dutch town of Haarlem, and under the flagstones I would find a great chest of gold. Quite ridiculous! I think you should go home to your good husband and forget your dreams," and he walked away down the street.

Kaatje could not really believe what she had heard but tired as she was, she went home again as fast as ever she could.

47

Hans was cross with her at first for going on such a fool's errand, but when she demanded he dig up the dairy floor he just laughed at her. So she picked up the spade and began digging by herself.

The pile of earth grew higher and higher, and Hans despaired for his clean dairy. But then the spade struck something metal. Hans and Kaatje peered down into the hole.

An old rusting chest lay on its side, and spilling out was a great pile of coins! Well, then they both dug away with both hands and soon there was a great pile of gold coins on the dairy floor, enough to keep them in great comfort for the rest of their days. They were content with their way of life so they stayed at the farm near the crossroads by the Old Inn outside the Dutch town of Haarlem, and Hans went every week to market with his cheeses. But Kaatje never remembered a single one of her dreams ever again.